D0511511

For Oscar X

OXFORD
UNIVERSITY PRESS

Great Clarendon Street, Oxford OX2 6DP

Oxford University Press is a department of the University of Oxford.
It furthers the University's objective of excellence in research, scholarship,
and education by publishing worldwide in

Oxford New York

Auckland Bangkok Buenos Aires Cape Town Chennai Dar es Salaam
Delhi Hong Kong Istanbul Karachi Kolkata Kuala Lumpur Madrid Melbourne
Mexico City Mumbai Nairobi São Paulo Shanghai Singapore Taipei Tokyo Toronto

Oxford is a registered trade mark of Oxford University Press
in the UK and in certain other countries

Text and illustrations © Joanne Partis 2003

The moral rights of the author/artist have been asserted

Database right Oxford University Press (maker)

First published 2003

All rights reserved. No part of this publication may be reproduced, stored in
a retrieval system, or transmitted, in any form or by any means, without the prior
permission in writing of Oxford University Press, or as expressly permitted by law,
or under terms agreed with the appropriate reprographics rights organization.
Enquiries concerning reproduction outside the scope of the above should be sent
to the Rights Department, Oxford University Press, at the address above

You must not circulate this book in any other binding or cover
and you must impose this same condition on any acquirer

British Library Cataloguing in Publication Data available

ISBN 0 19 279088 9 (hardback)
ISBN 0 19 272536 X (paperback)

3 5 7 9 10 8 6 4 2

Typeset in Diotima

Printed in Singapore by Imago

My Cat Just Sleeps

Joanne Partis

OXFORD
UNIVERSITY PRESS

My friends have all got fun cats.

They jump,

and chase,

and play

and hunt.

But my cat doesn't do any of those things.

My cat just sleeps.

George's cat climbs trees.
He can climb right up to the
highest branches and he
never, ever, falls.

But my cat won't even climb a small tree.

My cat just sleeps.

Harry's cat digs up worms
in the garden.

She likes carrying them around
in her mouth.

But my cat isn't interested in worms.

My cat just sleeps.

Molly's cat plays with the fish in her pond. She splashes with her paws, while she licks her lips.

But my cat doesn't like fishing.

My cat just sleeps.

I wish my cat was exciting.
But all he does
is snooze ...

and yawn ...

and purr.

He cuddles up
on my lap,

and he keeps my feet
warm at night.

My cat does LOTS of things!

I love my cat.

Purr
Purr
Purr

But I wish I knew why he is always so sleepy.